THE TORTILLA QUILT

Story ◆ Recipe ◆ Quilt Pattern

The Tortilla Quilt
Copyright 1996 Jane Tenorio-Coscarelli
Publisher: ¼ Inch Designs & Publishing
Copy Editor: Connie Culter
Translation Editor: Mark Koscielak
Technical Editor: Janet Neeper
Quilt Designer: Linda Sawery
Machine Quilting By: Arnette Jasperson
Quilt Photography By: Carina Woolrich Photography

Published By
¼ Inch Designs & Publishing
33255 Stoneman Street #B
Lake Elsinore Ca. 92530 USA

Library of Congress Cataloging Card Number: 96-92477
ISBN: HB 0-9653422-0-4
       PB 0-9653422-1-2

Printed in China
By Regent Publishing Services

10 9 8

In memory of my mother
Emma A. Tenorio
"NANA"
for all those rainy days
you filled with sunshine
and the smell of
homemade tortillas.

I will always remember...

My children Nicole and Dominic.
Be proud of your heritage...

My husband Bill of twenty years
for making me laugh...

My Friendship Quilters
and family who said
"You Can Do It"...

My co-workers and technical advisors...

A HEARTFELT THANK YOU
ENJOY

Janie

Note to the Reader
The purpose of our books is to introduce and expand Spanish vocabulary.
We do not intend to teach the rules of Spanish grammar, sentence structure, or verb use.
Therefore, all verbs that appear in the text are not conjugated in their proper form and are
represented by their unconjugated, or infinitive form. We chose to keep verbs in their
unconjugated form so that readers will become familiar with the root of a verb and be able to
recognize other forms of the verb by identifying the root. Our hope is that by introducing Spanish
vocabulary, readers will become interested in the Spanish language and will want to pursue
learning the language on a higher level. We hope that you enjoy our stories and find them a
valuable stepping stone to learning about another language and culture.

The Tortilla Quilt Story

By
Jane Tenorio-Coscarelli

Maria lived with her grandmother Lupita
abuela

on a large ranch in California. Lupita worked
rancho grande

as a cook for the Olson family. Maria would
familia

help her grandmother daily. She would rise

early in the morning to start her chores before
mañana

the rest of the family was up.

1

Maria would tend the chickens daily and

go out to the chicken coop to gather eggs to
pollera *huevos*
prepare breakfast for the Olson family.
desayuno
Grandmother Lupita would be busy making

tortillas.

Maria's best friend was Sarah Olson. She
amiga
was lucky to live with someone her own age.

The ranch was large and had many horses and
caballos
donkeys. Sarah and Maria would ride and
burros
play together all day.

5

After the evening meal, Maria would

watch Sarah sit and sew by lamp light with

sentarse   *luz*
her mother.   They were making a quilt

madre
together.   They would talk and laugh together.

Maria wanted so much to make a quilt too.

7

She would tell her grandmother about the

beautiful quilts Sarah and her mother were
bellas
making, but she knew she did not have all the

pretty colored fabric like Sarah. A quilt
bonita   *tela*
would be so expensive for her to make.

Lupita could see the disappointment on

Maria's face.
cara

9

One day, while making tortillas for the

morning meal, Maria's grandmother realized

she had a dozen flour and meal sacks in the

docena

pantry. She thought the sacks might work for

Maria's quilt.

She called Maria into the kitchen and sat

cocina

her at the table. Grandmother Lupita gave

mesa

Maria a square template of kindling wood to

leña

use as a pattern. Maria traced and cut the

cortó

square pieces out very carefully with scissors.

She would place them neatly on the table.

13

She was so excited about her quilt she had
to share it with her best friend Sarah. Sarah
saw the quilt of flour sacks and how hard
Maria was working on cutting the fabric.
Sarah told Maria she needed a little color in
                                        color
her quilt. So Sarah went to her mother for
                                        madre
help.

15

Mrs. Olson said she had some of Maria

and Sarah's dresses that they had outgrown.
vestidos
Sarah and Maria could cut them up for quilt

squares. The quilt began to grow and grow.

It now took up the whole table.

Soon Maria had to set it on the

kitchen floor. Sarah and Maria would spend
suelo de la cocina
hours playing with all the pieces, deciding

where each needed to be. Like a jigsaw

puzzle of fabric and memories, the pieces

began to fit together. Maria's birthday dress,
cumpleaños
Sarah's Christmas dress, a blouse with little
Navidad
flowers that was Maria's favorite. Each
flores
fabric square saying, remember me.

19

Soon the girls decided it was time to sew

the pieces together. Sarah brought out her

sewing basket. She gave Maria a needle,
canasta
thread, and a thimble. Maria tried to put the
hilo   *dedal*
thimble on her thumb. This made Sarah

laugh. She told Maria to put it on her other

finger. The thimble would help push the

needle through the fabric.

They sat by the fire and tenderly stitched
fuego
each piece together. Maria's grandmother

was so very proud of how hard the girls
orgullosa
worked together on the quilt top.

23

When they finished the top of the quilt,

Lupita put the black iron on the woodburning
plancha negra
stove. When it was hot enough, she pressed
estufa   *caliente*
the top nice and flat.

Then Sarah said they needed batting for

the quilt. She asked her mother if she could

help with Maria's quilt. Mrs. Olson went to

her sewing room and returned with some
cuarto
pieces of cotton batting. The girls could see
pedazos
some seeds in the cotton fabric. It would
semillas   *algodón*
make the quilt good and warm.

They happily stitched the pieces together.

For the backing of the quilt they stitched

together the rest of the flour sacks. You

harina

could see labels of all the different flour and

meal companies on the back of the quilt.

Lupita again heated the iron and pressed the

back nice and flat.

She then laid it on the kitchen floor. Then
puso   *suelo*
they laid the batting over the backing. Lastly,

they laid the pieced quilt on top. Sarah and

Maria took big basting stitches to hold the

quilt together so it would not move or slip

apart.

Mrs. Olson said Maria could use her big

wooden quilting frame. This was a special

honor for Maria's quilt, because it would
honor
remain in the Olson family parlor until they

finished quilting the quilt.

For many evenings the women of the
noches   *mujeres*
house---Maria, Sarah, Mrs. Olson, and even

Grandma Lupita---quilted on the quilt. Maria

quilted hearts in the squares because she loved
corazones
her quilt so. Sarah quilted feathers in the
plumas
borders because it reminded her of the ranch

chickens and how she and Maria would steal

their eggs. Mrs. Olson quilted hands because
manos
so many hands had worked on the quilt.

Lupita quilted angel wings because the girls
alas
were her little angels. They stitched and

laughed and told stories of the ranch. When
cuentos
they were done, Mrs. Olson showed Maria

how to bind the edge of her quilt.

35

When Maria finished the last stitches on

her quilt, the girls laid it on Sarah's white

iron bed. They picked out the colors of the
cama   *colores*
dresses they wore when they were little and

told stories of each different fabric. Sarah

asked Maria what she was going to do with

the quilt.

Maria wrapped it in paper and said,
papel
"follow me." Sarah followed her into the

kitchen. Maria's grandmother had just

finished making tortillas and was cleaning up.

Maria asked her to sit down for a
sentarse

minute. The girls stood next to each other

giggling. Maria hid the package behind her

back. Lupita asked what they were up to.

Maria handed her grandmother the package.
paquete

She asked what it was. "It's not my

birthday!"
cumpleaños

Maria said, "Go ahead, grandmother, open

it."

The girls watched as she unwrapped the

package. There was the quilt with all its
paquete
colors and fine quilting stitches. Maria told

her grandmother to read the back of the quilt.

In the corner, in Maria's finest embroidery
mejor
was stitched:

The Tortilla Quilt for Grandmother Lupita
From Her Angels
Maria and Sarah
1880

43

Maria's grandmother wrapped the quilt

around them both. With a tear in her eye, she
                              lágrima   *ojo*
hugged and kissed each on the forehead. She
      besó
said the tortilla quilt would keep her warm on

cold nights with memories of them both
  noches frías
growing up.

Maria now has the tortilla quilt and tells

her own daughter the stories of her childhood
hija
on the ranch and of how the tortilla quilt came

to be one day in her grandmother Lupita's
abuela
kitchen so many quilts ago. She reminds her

daughter that quilts not only warm the body,

but they also warm the heart. At this, she
corazón
remembered the tortilla quilt and smiled.
sonrió

THE END

GRANDMA LUPITA'S FLOUR TORTILLAS
TORTILLAS DE HARINA

4 cups flour	6 tablespoons shortening or oil
2 teaspoons salt	1 to 1¼ cups lukewarm water

Sift dry ingredients, add shortening, working it into the flour. Stir in 1 cup water and form into a ball; more water can be added if necessary, until bowl is clean of all dough. Knead well on floured board and make balls the size of an egg. Let them stand for 15 minutes; then roll out with rolling pin until they are salad plate size. Place on hot ungreased skillet or griddle on top of stove, cook for about 2 minutes on one side, then turn to other side and cook 1 minute longer. Serve freshly made or reheat later.

THE TORTILLA QUILT

"46 X 52"
Designer: Linda Sawrey

THE TORTILLA QUILT - INSTRUCTIONS
"46 x 54"
(Block Size 6" finished)

FABRIC REQUIREMENTS- 1/4 yd. of 11 different fabrics. This will give you extra, but for variety you will need that many fabrics.

FIRST BORDER- 1/4 yd. of fabric

SECOND BORDER- 3/4 yd. - if using a stripe as pictured, you will need 1 3/4 yd.

BACKING- 2 1/2 yd. (or piece leftover scraps of fabric)

BINDING- 1/2 yd. of fabric

From each fabric cut: (all measurements include 1/4" seam allowance)

       1 - 3 1/2" square (A)
       4 - 2 x 3 1/2 rectangle (B)
       4 - 2" squares (C)
       2 - 6 1/2 squares (alternate blocks)

PIECING: note all piecing uses 1/4" scam allowance.

Choose two fabrics and combine as shown below in block piecing diagram.

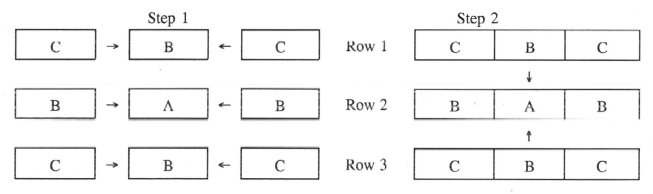

After each unit is sewn together, sew Row 1, 2, and 3 together.

Make 21 blocks. Alternate blocks with 6 1/2 solid squares refering to photo.

This quilt is 6 blocks across and 7 blocks down.

FIRST BORDER- Cut 1 1/2" strips and sew to top and bottom of center. Then sew strips to sides. Square up corners. Press.

SECOND BORDER- Cut 4 1/2" strips and add to quilt as in first border. Press.

BASTE- Lay flat - backing, batting, and quilt top. Baste to hold in place.

QUILTING- Quilt is quilted in the ditch around each block. Quilt patterns are in each solid block.

BINDING- Cut 5 - 2 1/2" strips. Sew together end to end. Fold in half wrong sides together. Press. Sew to top of quilt, raw edges out. Press, turn, and tack to back of quilt. Refer to basic quilting book for instructions. Press. Add label to back of quilt.

Quilting Patterns

Heart

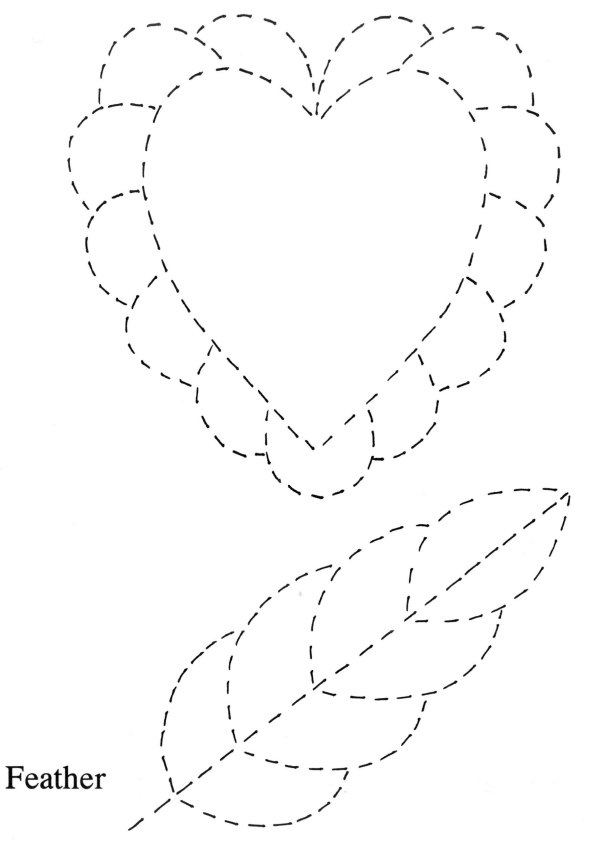

Feather

Quilting Patterns

Hand

Angelwings

Other Products from ¼ Inch Designs & Publishing

Books
The Tortilla Quilt
The Tamale Quilt
The Ants / Las Hormigas
The Piñata Quilt

Quilt Patterns

Coffee Girls	And Baby Makes Three	Raggedy Pals
Cat's Pajamas	Material Garden	Teas the Season
Deck the Cat	A Box of Chocolates	Heart of My Heart
Okay Corral	Roller Ghoster	Harvest Moon
Fall Friends	Winter Willie	Spring Seeds
Summer Picnic	Cooped Up	Mending Patches

Doll Patterns
Maria Doll   Quilt-a-beast Doll

Other Products
Quilt-a-beast Mugs & Tote Bags
Fall & Winter Note Card Sets

**For author visits, lectures, workshop information
or to order contact:
¼ Inch Designs & Publishing
33255 Stoneman Street #B Lake Elsinore Ca. 92530
Phone 909 609-3309 Fax 909 609-3369 E-mail:Quarteri@aol.com
Visit Our Website www.quarterinchpublishing.com
For a catalog send a SASE**